The Impossible Patriotism Project

by **Linda Skeers**

pictures by **Ard Hoyt**

PUFFIN BOOKS

Bob, whose belief in me never wavered—this is for you
—L.S.

To our troops both home and abroad who sacrifice so much
to ensure our many freedoms. Thank you all.
—A.H.

PUFFIN BOOKS • Published by the Penguin Group • Penguin Young Readers Group, 345 Hudson Street, New York, New York 10014, U.S.A. • Penguin Group (Canada), 90 Eglinton Avenue East, Suite 700, Toronto, Ontario, Canada M4P 2Y3 (a division of Pearson Penguin Canada Inc.) • Penguin Books Ltd, 80 Strand, London WC2R 0RL, England • Penguin Ireland, 25 St Stephen's Green, Dublin 2, Ireland (a division of Penguin Books Ltd) • Penguin Group (Australia), 250 Camberwell Road, Camberwell, Victoria 3124, Australia (a division of Pearson Australia Group Pty Ltd) • Penguin Books India Pvt Ltd, 11 Community Centre, Panchsheel Park, New Delhi - 110 017, India • Penguin Group (NZ), 67 Apollo Drive, Rosedale, North Shore 0632, New Zealand (a division of Pearson New Zealand Ltd) • Penguin Books (South Africa) (Pty) Ltd, 24 Sturdee Avenue, Rosebank, Johannesburg 2196, South Africa • Registered Offices: Penguin Books Ltd, 80 Strand, London WC2R 0RL, England • First published in the United States of America by Dial Books for Young Readers, a division of Penguin Young Readers Group, 2007 • Published by Puffin Books, a division of Penguin Young Readers Group, 2009 • 1 2 3 4 5 6 7 8 9 10 • Text copyright © Linda Skeers, 2007 • Pictures copyright © Ard Hoyt, 2007 • All rights reserved

THE LIBRARY OF CONGRESS HAS CATALOGED THE DIAL BOOKS FOR YOUNG READERS EDITION AS FOLLOWS: Skeers, Linda. • The impossible patriotism project / by Linda Skeers ; pictures by Ard Hoyt. • p. cm.Summary: Caleb has a hard time coming up with a way to symbolize patriotism for Presidents' Day until he realizes that his dad, who is away from home in the military, is what patriotism is all about. • ISBN: 978-0-8037-3138-7 (hc)
[1. Patriotism—Fiction. 2. Schools—Fiction. 3. Presidents' Day—Fiction] I. Hoyt, Ard, ill. II. Title. • PZ7.S62585Imp 2007 • [E]—dc22 • 2005024774
Puffin Books ISBN 978-0-14-241391-3 • Manufactured in China • Designed by Jasmin Rubero • Text set in Adobe Caslon

Caleb slumped in his chair. Mrs. Perkins had just announced the class projects for Presidents' Day. "Make something showing patriotism?" he mumbled. That was way too hard.

"For Parents' Night tomorrow we'll decorate the classroom and have a party to display your work," Mrs. Perkins said.

The class cheered. They loved celebrations. Especially if it meant cupcakes.

But not even the thought of a cupcake with extra frosting and sprinkles could cheer up Caleb.

Everyone got busy. Everyone but Caleb.

He didn't know where to start. Patriotism wasn't something you could draw, like a tree or a spaceship or a crocodile. He was good at drawing crocodiles. Why couldn't they be having a Crocodile Celebration?

Caleb walked around the room to see what everyone was doing.

"I'm going to make a papier-mâché Liberty Bell," said Hannah. "I touched the Liberty Bell once on vacation. I'm pretty sure that's about as patriotic as you can get."

Caleb had never seen the Liberty Bell except in pictures. And he wasn't good at papier-mâché. Everything ended up looking like lumpy mashed potatoes.

Besides, the Liberty Bell was Hannah's idea.

"Hey, Kareem," Caleb asked, "what are you going to make?"

Kareem stopped sorting through his crayons. "A map of the United States," he said. "Each state will be a different color. When I grow up and become president, I'll have to know where all the states are—even New Mexico and Iowa. I'll hang this map in the White House so I can keep them straight." He started coloring. "You have to be patriotic to be president. I think it's a law."

Caleb still didn't have an idea for his project and wondered why he should bother. His dad couldn't come to Parents' Night anyway.

"What are you working on?" Caleb asked Jake.

"Writing a poem about America," Jake said. "I don't think anything rhymes with America, though. Maybe I'll write a poem about the states." He started writing. "Wonder what's more patriotic—crates, gates, or skates?"

Caleb slouched in his chair and frowned. Why had Mrs. Perkins picked patriotism for their projects?

He looked around the room. Everyone was hard at work.

Except Molly. Caleb leaned over to her. "Can't think of an idea either?" he asked her.

"No, I have a great idea! I'll dress up as the Statue of Liberty and have fireworks go off over my head." She scrunched up her forehead. "Maybe I'll hand out sparklers . . ."

Fireworks? Sparklers? Caleb groaned. Maybe he could tell Mrs. Perkins he would be sick on Parents' Night. He was coming down with a cold. Or a broken leg.

That night Caleb sat on his bed. "I wish Dad were here to help me with this project. He would know that patriotism is more than a map or a statue." He sighed. "But how do I show that?" Suddenly Caleb smiled. Maybe his dad could help him after all.

The next day the class hung lots of red, white, and blue streamers. Every desk held a small American flag. Projects were set up all over the room. Molly was pouting. Mrs. Perkins had said *no* fireworks and *no* sparklers. Not even a little one with barely any fizzle.

Bald Eagle

Caleb set a big poster board next to his desk. His project was done.

That night the celebration started with a sing-along in the gym and a speech by the principal. Then the students and parents filed down the hall and into the classrooms.

Molly had draped herself with a green sheet and was holding a flashlight. "Awesome Statue of Liberty," said Caleb.

"Would've been better with fireworks," she grumbled, but then Caleb saw her smile proudly and hold her flashlight up a little higher.

Kareem's map was incredible! He'd mixed colors together so all fifty states were different. Georgia was a color Caleb had never seen before.

Hannah's papier-mâché Liberty Bell was nice.
And hardly lumpy at all.

"What's going on over *there*?" asked Caleb's mom. A small crowd had gathered around Caleb's desk.

"It's my project," whispered Caleb as they squeezed through the crowd.

"Who is it?" asked Molly.

"That's a picture of my dad in his uniform," Caleb said proudly. "Patriotism means going away from your family even if you have to miss Parents' Night. It means keeping everyone in the United States safe." He smiled and gently touched the picture. "My dad taught me to love my country.

My *dad* is patriotism."

"He would be so proud of you," whispered Caleb's mom. She hugged him right in front of everyone.

Kareem unpinned his map from the bulletin board. He took a black crayon and wrote *THANK YOU* in the corner. "Can you send this to your dad?" he asked.

"Don't you need it for when you're president?" Caleb asked.

"I'll make another one," he said. "After I get more crayons."

Caleb tucked the map under his arm and looked around the room. His project had turned out fine. He couldn't wait to tell his dad about it.